Figler
My Imaginary Friend

Story by Erica Taylor

Pictures by Mr. Piecrust

Parkhurst Brothers Publishers
Marion, Michigan

www.parkhurstbrothers.com

Parkhurst Brothers books are distributed to the trade through the Chicago Distribution Center, and may be ordered through Ingram Book Company, Baker & Taylor, Follett Library Resources and other book industry wholesalers. To order from Chicago Distribution Center, phone 1-800-621-2736 or send a fax to 800-621-8476. Copies of this and other Parkhurst Brothers Inc., Publishers titles are available to organizations and corporations for purchase in quantity by contacting Special Sales Department at our home office location, listed on our web site. Manuscript submission guidelines for this publishing company are available at our web site.

Printed in the United States of America

First Edition, 2014

2014 2015 2016 2017 2018   12 10 9 8 7 6 5 4 3 2 1

Library of Congress Cataloging-in-Publication Data

Taylor, Erica (Erica C.), 1982-
Figler : my imaginary friend / story by Erica Taylor ; illustration by Mr. Piecrust. -- First edition.
pages cm
Summary: A kindergartner describes Figler, a very real imaginary friend.
ISBN 978-1-62491-021-0 (alk. paper) -- ISBN 978-1-62491-012-8
[1. Imaginary playmates--Fiction.] I. Mr. Piecrust, illustrator. II. Title.
PZ7.T21266Fig 2014
[E]--dc23
2014019940

This book is printed on archival-quality paper that meets requirements of the American National Standard for Information Sciences, Permanence of Paper, Printed Library Materials, ANSI Z39.48-1984.

Cover and page design: Susan Harring

Cover and text illustration: Mr. Piecrust

Acquired for Parkhurst Brothers Publishers

And edited by: Ted Parkhurst

Author photo by: Cindy Momchilov

052014

This book is dedicated to my family: Jermain, our children Nia Jay, Tyra, Laila, Jace, and Lil' Main, for unconditional love and never-ending memories; to my parents and siblings for love, laughter and loyalty. Laila, thank you for inspiring me to write about your darling personality and your perfect imaginary friend, Figler. Mr. Parkhurst, thank you for giving me a chance.

My mom says that Figler is my imaginary friend.
But Figler's real to me—everything I am within.

Figler is brave and courageous.

He isn't afraid of dogs.

Timid and curious, I watch them
chase a cat through the fog.

Figler wears yellow big kid pants.

He doesn't wet the bed.

For little me, it's pull-ups—
blue, purple, and red.

Figler can see grasshoppers
near and planets *far.*
Only with glasses can I see
Venus, the moon, and stars.

Figler is a big boy;
he can tie his brown shoes.

My hands are small.
Velcro will *have to do*.

Figler is a genius!

He reads five-letter words.

As he reads,

I look at pictures of bluebirds.

Figler is an artist. He draws
tall giraffes and taller mountains.

My scribble-scrabble is an
evening rainbow in a fountain!

My superhero glasses
are just the right size

To see the love in
my friend Figler's eyes.

He is *not* my imagination.

Figler's as real as a tree.

Whenever I'm scared,
Figler makes me feel free.

Figler is not my imagination.
He is my best friend forever—
No matter when I need him,
he's always in the mirror!

Teachable Moments in
Figler: My Imaginary Friend

By the author, a third-grade teacher...and mom!

Lesson:
Concepts of Self in Society

Abstract:
Concepts of self in society **is a unit that integrates English language arts, poetry, visual arts, and self-representation. This unit was written using the book** *Figler: My Imaginary Friend* **by Erica Taylor.** *Concepts of self in society* **provides reading, writing, speaking, collaborative learning activities to develop an awareness of self-perception and self-esteem. In addition, children are given the opportunity to create original art projects and present a dramatic interpretation to compliment** *Figler: My Imaginary Friend. Concepts of self in society* **is a natural, enjoyable and creative approach to self-discovery.**

Concept Objectives:

A. **Students will develop an appreciation for poetry.**

B. **Students will develop a sense of self-discovery.**

Lesson Plan: "Figler My Imaginary Friend"

Vocabulary Words:

<u>Imagination</u>: the ability to come up with mental pictures or new and creative ideas that is not real

<u>Author</u>: someone who creates or writes something

<u>Illustrator</u>: an artist who draws the pictures for books

<u>Friend</u>: a person that you like, with whom you talk or spend time

<u>Coward</u>: a person who lacks courage

<u>Courage</u>: the bravery and/or strength to do something that could be dangerous

<u>Confidence</u>: to have faith, trust, and self-assurance

<u>Self-esteem</u>: to have belief and pride in yourself

<u>Rhyme</u>: rhyme is a poem composed of lines with similar ending sounds ("bike" and "like)

<u>Easel</u>: a standing frame used for holding something (art work or pictures)

<u>Goals</u>: an objective to be achieved. (i.e.: My goal is to make all A's and B's)

<u>Role model</u>: someone who others admire, someone who has traits or talents that you want to be like

<u>Lonely</u>: being alone, not near other people; to feel unhappy

<u>Brave</u>: to have courage

<u>Timid</u>: shy and fearful

<u>Cautious</u>: to be aware and alert to danger

<u>Intelligent</u>: someone who is smart

<u>Genius</u>: someone with an amazing mental or creative ability

<u>Weak</u>: to lack strength

<u>Strong</u>: someone with a lot of power. The ability to do a task very well

<u>Narrator</u>: the person who tells the story

Procedures/Activities:

1. Teacher will read the title, "Figler: My Imaginary Friend." Students will make predictions about the story.

2. Teacher will read "Figler: My Imaginary Friend" aloud. Students will ask questions about the story and the illustrations.

3. Teacher will ask students to name things they have in common with Figler.

4. Teacher will give each student construction paper to make "fold-able vocabulary" worksheet.

5. Teacher will go over and discuss vocabulary words.

6. Teacher will ask students to describe how each vocabulary is used in the story.

7. Teacher will discuss rhyming words. Students will discuss and go over rhyming words that are presented in the story, "Figler: My Imaginary Friend".

8. Teacher will go to the board and ask students to help her with other rhyming words (can/ran, cat/hat, see/be, pain/rain, etc…)

9. Teacher will pass out "Figler" books (Oxford Linen Clear Front Report Cover and 10-15 copier pages). Teacher will tell the students they will be the author and the illustrator of their work. This will be in the form of poetry. Teacher will explain to the student they can use the rhyming words in the story, on the board, or create new ones on their own.

10. On the board the teacher will write, "What do I want to be when I grow up and how do I plan to accomplish my goal?"

11. When students have completed, they will put their work in the report cover.

12. Teacher will ask students to read their work and display their work.

Comprehension Questions:

1. Who is the author of "Figler My Imaginary Friend"?

2. Who is the illustrator of "Figler My Imaginary Friend?

3. Name five adjectives that describe the Figler.

Skill Objectives:

C. The students will listen attentively to the reading of *Figler: My Imaginary Friend.*

D. The students will discuss similarities and differences they have with the main character Figler.

E. The students will discuss, "What are you afraid of?"

F. The students will write about, "What do you want to be when you grow up?"

G. The students will discuss how they plan to achieve their goals.

H. The students will discuss Figler's confidence.

I. The students will express ideas through original art work.

J. The students will write "Why do I believe in myself?"

K. Students will develop an extensive vocabulary.

Resources:
Taylor, Erica. *Figler: My Imaginary Friend*, Parkhurst Brothers, Marion, Michigan, 2014.
ISBN: 9-781-62491-021-0

4. Name five adjectives that describe the narrator.

5. What is Figler chasing? Where is Figler chasing it?

6. Is Figler afraid of dogs?

7. What color are Figler's big boy pants?

8. What does the narrator wear to bed? What color are they?

9. Does Figler have accidents at night?

10. Name some things that Figler draws.

11. What does the narrator call his drawing?

12. What can Figler see near?

13. What can Figler see far?

14. Name a planet that was named in the story.

15. On page 15, what type of bird is in the picture?

Critical thinking:

Why do you think there is a monkey throughout the story?

At what point in the story does the narrator realize he can conquer all the things his imaginary friend Figler can?

What is the difference in the narrator and Figler's glasses?

Does the narrator lack confidence? Why?

Who is the narrator's role model? Why?

In the beginning of the book, does the narrator think he can conquer the same things as Figler?

What does the narrator means when he says, "No matter when I need him, he's always in the mirror."?

Write a paragraph to tell who is your friend (real or imaginary) and why.

Does Figler believe in himself? Explain.